10/0/
24.95

of Reptiles

ge of Mammals

ago

Palaeozoic Era (P
begins 570 millio

Mesozoic Era (Mi
begins 240 million

Cenozoic Era (Rec
begins 65 million

Today

Cretaceous Period (140-65 mya)

Dinosaurs disappear 65 million years ago

DISCOVERIES IN PALAEONTOLOGY

ALBERTOSAURUS

Death of a Predator

MONIQUE KEIRAN

ROYAL TYRRELL MUSEUM

RAINCOAST BOOKS

Vancouver

First published in 1999 by
Raincoast Books
8680 Cambie Street
Vancouver, B.C.
V6P 6M9
(604) 323-7100
www.raincoast.com

1 2 3 4 5 6 7 8 9 10

Canadian Cataloguing in Publication Data
Keiran, Monique
  Albertosaurus
  (Discoveries in palaeontology, ISSN 1489-7784; no. 1)
  ISBN 1-55192-258-4

1. Albertosaurus. 2. Paleontology—Alberta. I. Title. II. Series.
QE862.S3K45 1999   567.912   C99-910492-6

Portrait of J.B. Tyrrell courtesy of the Geological Survey of Canada (photo number GSC 201735-A).
Archival photo, p.8: C. Sternberg photo published with the permission of the Canadian Museum of Nature, Ottawa.
Cover Photography by Merle Prosofsky
Design by Ruth Linka
Colour separations by ChromaTech Inc., Vancouver, B.C., Canada
Prepress by DPI, Vancouver, B.C., Canada

The Canada Council for the Arts since 1957 | Le Conseil des Arts du Canada depuis 1957

Raincoast Books gratefully acknowledges the support of the Government of Canada, through the Book Publishing Industry Development Program, the Canada Council for the Arts, and the Department of Canadian Heritage. We also acknowledge the assistance of the Province of British Columbia, through the British Columbia Arts Council.

Printed in Canada

Acknowledgements

Many thanks to Dr. Stephen Godfrey for initiating the project, working on the manuscript, assembling information and providing his artwork.

· Illustrations: Dr. Stephen Godfrey; Javier Palomino; Donna Sloan; Monique Keiran.

Photos from the Royal Tyrrell Museum of Palaeontology archives: Monica Nash; Linda Moore; Colin Orthner; Merle Prosofsky, Kathy Simpkins, Monique Keiran

Other photos: Geological Survey of Canada, Natural Resources Canada; Travel Alberta; Monique Keiran; Canadian Museum of Nature; Merle Prosofsky. Cover photo by Merle Prosofsky.

Scientific Advisors: Dr. Philip Currie (Dinosaur Palaeontology); Dr. David Eberth (Sedimentary Geology); Dr. Don Brinkman (Vertebrate Palaeontology) and Dr. Dennis Braman (Palaeobotany)

Also instrumental to the project are: Dr. Bruce Naylor; Monty Reid; Marty Hickie; Scott Mair; Darren Tanke; Dennis Lister; Clive Coy; Lindsay Cook; Vien Lam; Andy Neuman; Tim Schowalter; Jackie Wilke; Paul Salvatore. From Raincoast Books: Brian Scrivener; Kevin Williams; Ruth Linka.

The Royal Tyrrell Museum thanks the Alberta Historical Resources Foundation and PoCo Petroleums Limited for helping make this book possible.

The plants, dinosaurs and other animals illustrated in this book reflect the fossil record of Dinosaur Provincial Park, Alberta. Stories and illustrations have been reviewed and approved by scientists at the Royal Tyrrell Museum of Palaeontology.

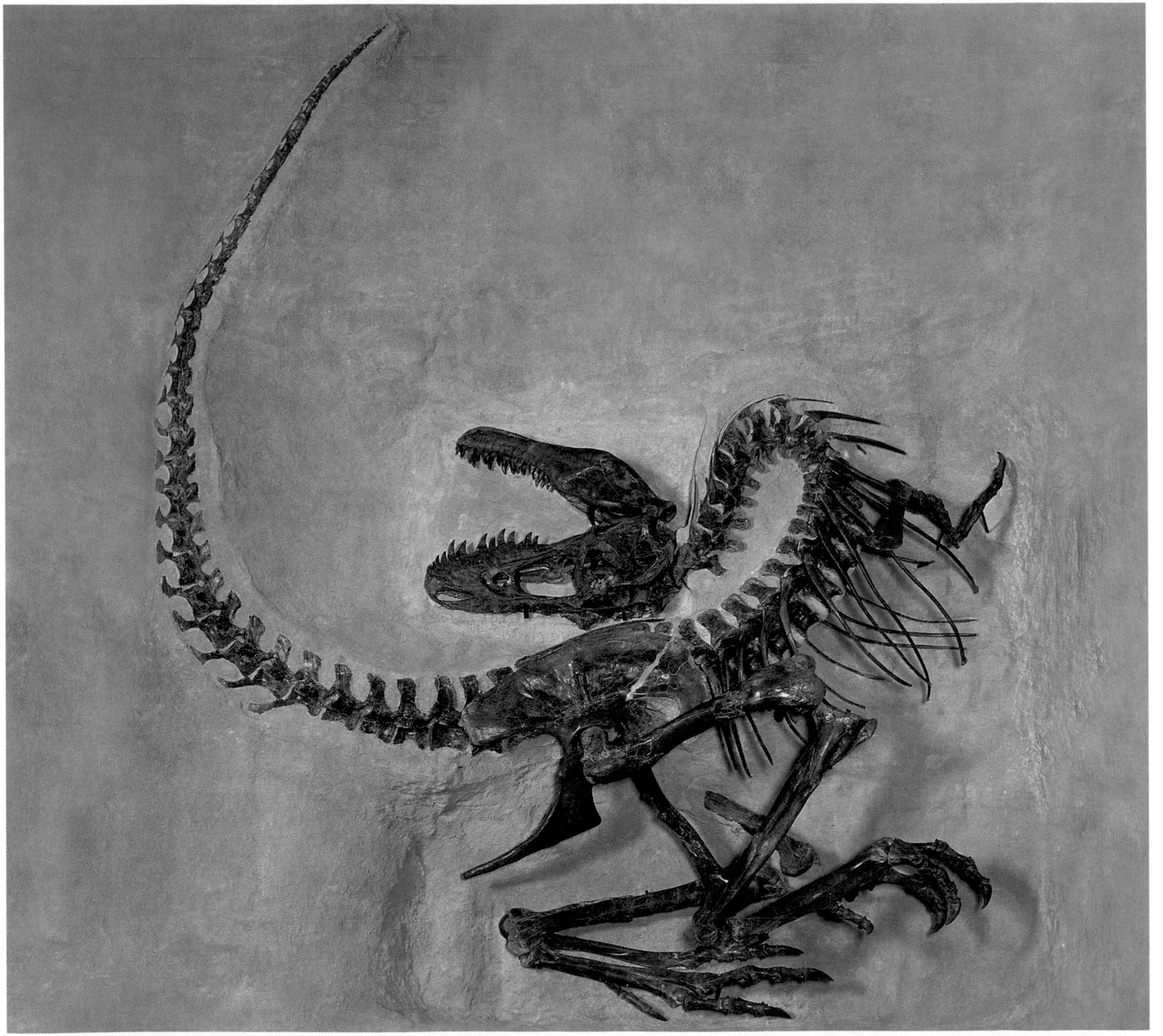

Merle Prosofsky

TABLE OF CONTENTS

Hidden within the stark, haunting landscape of southern Alberta's Dinosaur Provincial Park are some of the world's best-preserved dinosaur fossils.

TODAY: DINOSAUR PROVINCIAL PARK

AS YOU TRAVEL ACROSS SOUTHERN ALBERTA ON the TransCanada Highway, the prairie stretches away on all sides. The undulating plains of golden wheat and barley on the way to Dinosaur Provincial Park give no hint of what awaits you on your arrival. It isn't until you turn off at the park viewpoint and emerge into the unrelenting summer heat that the sun-baked remains of an ancient world can be seen.

At your feet are stone slopes that entomb thousands of creatures that are millions of years old. The hills are worn by wind and water, carved by every rainfall and snowmelt into intricate towers, steep-sided mounds and narrow, runnell-cliffed valleys. Baked-brown grasses, dusty green sagebrush and prairie wildflowers carpet the hilltops and drape over the sides.

In the distance is the green swath bordering the Red Deer River. Stately cottonwood trees and shrubby willows grow on the banks of the river. Thickets yield saskatoon berries, buffalo berries and chokecherries that, at the height of summer, feed songbirds and squirrels.

Cutting through the park's parched badlands, the Red Deer River is an oasis for plants and animals. The diversity of wildlife and abundance of dinosaur fossils led to the park's designation as an UNESCO World Heritage Site in 1979.

This is Dinosaur Provincial Park. Where dinosaurs once roamed, mule deer now make their home. Jackrabbits and snowshoe hares dodge owls and hawks. Rattlesnakes and bull snakes sun themselves on rock ledges. Porcupines nibble on twigs in the trees, and families of beavers constantly try damming narrow Little Sandhill Creek. From overhead comes the whoop of the common snipe and buzz of the nighthawk, and from the grasslands around you comes the sawing of grasshoppers.

If the wind is blowing from the right direction, you may hear the distant stutter of a jackhammer.

It is summer, and palaeontology field crews are hard at work removing overburden to excavate dinosaur bones. More than 40 species of dinosaurs have emerged from the canyon walls of Dinosaur Provincial Park. Thousands of fossils have found their way from this dusty cut in the prairie to museums and research institutes

C. STERNBERG

Dinosaur Provincial Park has drawn palaeontologists since the turn of the century. The Great Canadian Dinosaur Rush, from 1911 to 1917, saw boxcar-loads of fossils leave the park for museums and universities around the world.

around the world. London, Paris, New York, Buenos Aires, Los Angeles, Chicago, Ottawa, Toronto... all house the bones of animals that once lived in what is now Dinosaur Provincial Park. Since the 1970s, the fossils have stayed closer to the park – showcased at the Royal Tyrrell Museum of Palaeontology in Drumheller, Alberta.

The specimen that today's crew is collecting may be the leg bone of a **theropod**, one of the meat-eating dinosaurs that hunted here 75 million years ago. It is unlikely that more than one or two of the animal's bones will be found. Complete, **articulated** skeletons of any kind of dinosaur are unusual. Complete, articulated skeletons of meat-eating dinosaurs are almost never found. Of the thousands and thousands of fossils that have been excavated from Dinosaur Provincial Park by scientists during the last 100 years, fewer than 500 have been complete or nearly complete skeletons. Of these, only about one-tenth have been theropods.

One of the best of these is the juvenile *Albertosaurus*.

From the hill above Little Sandhill Creek, a panorama of Dinosaur Provincial Park stretches towards the horizon. Most of the park is classified as a Restricted Area – off limits to all but park staff and authorized scientists and their crews.

1991: DISCOVERY

PALAEONTOLOGIST PHILIP CURRIE WAS PROSPECTing in the south fork of Little Sandhill Coulee in Dinosaur Provincial Park on that Tuesday at the end of July in 1991, when he noticed a weathered, fractured bone sticking out of the ground.

Having studied thousands of dinosaur bones throughout his career, Currie immediately recognised this fossil. It was a dinosaur's **astragalus**, one of the ankle bones.

Chance plays a big role in finding fossils. Even seasoned palaeontologists like Philip Currie, one of the world's authorities on meat-eating dinosaurs, never knows when fractures fossil bone will lead them to a significant specimen.

That's when he started second guessing himself.

"My first instinct," he says, "was that it belonged to a theropod. Then I rationalized that that was extremely unlikely, and that it had to belong to a **hadrosaur** – one of the plant-eating dinosaurs – because they are so much more common."

Without spending more time examining the fossil, Currie marked the site on his map and instructed palaeontological technician Darren Tanke, who was working nearby, to collect the hadrosaur astragalus right away.

PART 1

75 Million Years Ago

The young dinosaur banged her nose against the hole in her eggshell. She fought to straighten her body curled within the confines of the space. She chipped at the hole, widening it just enough to grasp the edge with her toes and causing cracks to spiderweb around the surface. Large pieces of shell broke off as she poked at the hole. One big, straining push broke the shell in half. The young dinosaur tumbled into the nest.

Panting from her exertions, she opened large, blinking eyes to a warm and colourful world. The setting sun washed the landscape and tinted the clouds of steam evaporating from the sandy ground. To the northeast, a rainbow arced against a backdrop of storm clouds. The tall sycamore tree standing by the hatchling's home rustled in the breeze, showering water drops on the nest. A large drop splashed onto her nose, and she jerked her head back in surprise.

Around her, her nest mates peered about, exploring their home and becoming acquainted with siblings. Some still fought to free themselves from their half-metre-long shells, poking their claws and noses through the cracks.

Suddenly, behind her, bushes rustled and twigs snapped. Alarmed, she spun around to see a giant lizard dart out from the ferns, grab one of her nest mates, and disappear into the greenery. The young dinosaur twisted her head frantically, confused by the lingering stench of the lizard and the smell of blood.

From nearby came a thunderous roar. The young dinosaur scrambled to the edge of the nest and watched as, through the trees, the towering form of an adult tyrannosaur appeared, carrying the limp, bleeding body of a small hadrosaur in its jaws. The huge carnivore bounded across the clearing. Bending, it deposited the carcass by the nest and tore it apart with its teeth.

It turned and lowered its enormous snout towards the young dinosaur and her nest mates. The adult sniffed and snorted at the babies.

It was their mother, bringing their first meal.

The young dinosaur and her siblings tore into the meat.

The badlands of Dinosaur Provincial Park are made of layers of sandstone, shale, mudstone and coal formed 75 million years ago, and weathered by thousands of years of erosion.

Evidence in the Rocks

Hidden in today's landscapes are stories of ancient environments. The badlands of Dinosaur Provincial Park tell tales of ancient rivers and ponds, of estuaries, deltas and flood plains, of forests and swamps. Thick grey sandstones, reddish siltstones, layers of coal and fragments of volcanic rock all provide clues to the past. These rocks form what is called the Dinosaur Park Formation, a succession of rock layers up to 80 metres thick.

By studying these rocks, scientists have determined they are made of sand and silt carried by rivers from the ancient beginnings of the Rocky Mountains in eastern British Columbia, 76.5 to 74.5 million years ago. Some of the sediments were carried more than 900 kilometres. Thick deposits were laid down during storms, floods and tidal surges. Over millions of years, the accumulated sediments turned into the rock layers we see today.

The fossils in these rocks are remnants of an ancient, tropical world, home to many plants and animals. It was a time when there were only two seasons – wet and wetter. Crocodile, champsosaur and turtle fossils indicate temperatures in Dinosaur Provincial Park at that time were similar to those of the southern United States today – ranging from 14° to 35°C during the day. The whole world was warmer than it is now, and temperature differences across the globe less extreme. At the North Pole, which was located in the Yukon-Alaska region, the climate resembled that of present-day Vancouver and Seattle.

Long days of summer sunshine fuelled the growth of plants on the plain. Herbivorous dinosaurs fed on plants that included conifers, gingkoes and ferns. Small mammals and birds ate seeds and the fruit of flowering plants. In the fall, plant growth slowed as days became shorter.

Recent studies by Royal Tyrrell Museum of Palaeontology scientist Dave Eberth indicate the coastal plain was subject to regular monsoons and occasional hurricanes. Eberth speculates that as the days became shorter in winter, cool air over the western highlands would flow down across the coastal plain and meet the warm, humid air over the sea. As happens today over large bodies of warm water, the different air masses would circle around each other, fuelled by more warm air rising from the surface of the sea. If the system picked up enough energy, it would develop into a hurricane, and spin towards the coast, hammering it with rain and wind, and wreaking terrible damage.

The large amounts of sediment eroded and then deposited during the storms sometimes buried entire animal carcasses, protecting them from weathering and destruction, and allowing them to fossilize. This ancient environment set the stage for Dinosaur Provincial Park's fame – to date, 40 species of dinosaurs and almost 500 intact dinosaur skeletons have been discovered there.

Because of these remarkable fossil resources, the park was designated an UNESCO World Heritage Site in 1979.

The first Europeans to encounter the eroded terrain of some western North American river valleys were French explorers. Impeded by the mazes of hills and canyons, the rock that became buttery slick when wet, the clouds of biting insects and the lack of shelter from the sun, they labelled the terrain les terres mauvaises à traverser – bad lands to travel through – giving rise to the term badlands.

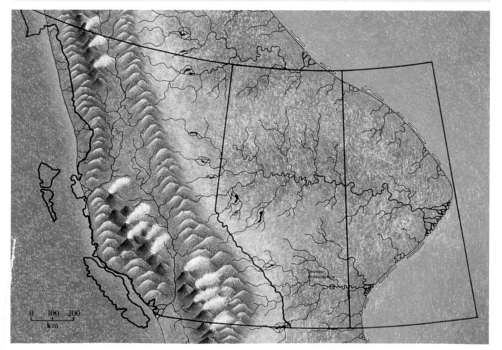

Drifting continents, receding sea levels and four recurring ice ages have changed the look of western North America in the 75 million years since Albertosaurus lived here.

There's no telling what a bit of fossilized dinosaur bone on the ground can lead to. This fractured and eroded bone led technician Darren Tanke (right) and palaeontologist Philip Currie to a complete, articulated skeleton.

Tanke couldn't find the hadrosaur astragalus that Currie had directed him to, but he did find one belonging to a **tyrannosaur**. Assuming that Currie had said "hadrosaur" when he meant "tyrannosaur," he went to work.

As he uncovered the ankle bone, he found it was attached to a leg bone. And another bone. And another…. Tanke became more and more excited – tyrannosaur bones are unusual, but articulated tyrannosaur bones are extremely rare. He started excavating around the fossils to determine the extent of the specimen.

When Currie returned to the site at the end of the day, Tanke presented him with the uncovered astragalus… attached to some foot bones and complete, articulated leg bones – all belonging to a small tyrannosaur.

"I have a really good feeling about this one," Tanke told Currie.

How Many Herbivores Does It Take to Feed a Carnivore?

Nobody knows how many species of dinosaurs there were, let alone how many individuals the ancient ecosystems could support. Surveys of collected fossils are misleading; many early dinosaur hunters collected only the biggest or best-preserved specimens, and left the rest. Although modern palaeontologists try to account for all kinds of fossils found, they still must deal with preservational biases – not every animal is preserved as a fossil.

Scientists estimate dinosaur populations based on the fossil record and on knowledge of modern animals. Every predator requires a stable and abundant population of prey to support itself – to hunt, to scavenge and to eat. One problem is that palaeontologists differ as to whether dinosaurs were warm-blooded or cold-blooded animals. The number of individuals an ecosystem can support differs for warm- and cold-blooded animals. Among animals today, the ratio of herbivore prey to warm-blooded carnivores of similar size is about 20 to one, and about half that for cold-blooded carnivores.

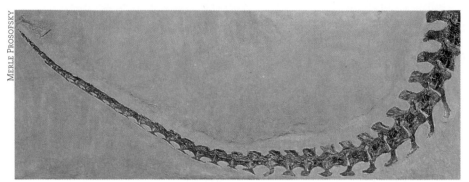

Millimetres long and millimetres across, the last tiny vertebra on the juvenile tyrannosaur's tail was collected. In total, the animal has more than 40 vertebrae in its 2.5-metre-long tail.

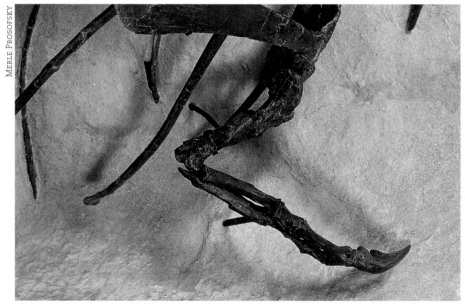

Finding the dinosaur's arm bones articulated ended a decades-long debate among palaeontolgists about how a tyrannosaur's arm fit together. It provides scientists with information on the range of movement and flexibility of the animal's arms.

As more and more bones of the animal appeared during the weeks following the discovery, excitement built among the field crew. More foot bones were found. Along a small wash to the side, a technician identified rib ends and hip bones. It began to look like most of the animal was there.

The animal's right arm was found with all its bones in place. It is the best articulated tyrannosaur arm ever found in Dinosaur Provincial Park. In previous discoveries, arm bones had always been found scattered, and palaeontologists were never sure exactly how the bones fit together in relation to one another. This dinosaur's arm ends the debate.

The tail was found. It, too, represents a first in palaeontology. The tail of this tyrannosaur skeleton is complete, right to the last tiny vertebra – only millimetres long and millimetres across. The three last vertebrae together measure only one centimetre long.

The bones indicated the specimen was small for *Albertosaurus*, measuring only about five metres long. Its size and proportions tell us the animal was young when it died – making this discovery of a rare, articulated meat-eating dinosaur even more unusual.

But was there a skull? Skulls are important discoveries. Using a dinosaur's skull, scientists can determine the animal's species and diet.

Two weeks later, the field crew uncovered a set of gaping jaws near the spot where the ankle

The juvenile Albertosaurus site in Little Sandhill Coulee was fairly accessible, as dinosaur quarries go. There was little overburden to remove, there were no cliffs to climb to the site, and there was room to move around the specimen. Heat stroke, sunstroke and dehydration were the biggest risks.

bone had lain. The rest of a remarkably preserved skull followed within days. Tanke had been sitting on the skull – cushioned by several centimetres of sandstone – the day he excavated the ankle bone.

Buried just centimetres below the fossilized ankle bone that had caught Philip Currie's attention were the dinosaur's gaping jaws.

One BIG, Hungry Family...

The dinosaur is Albertosaurus libratus. A member of the tyrannosaur family, its cousins include Tyrannosaurus rex and Desplesosaurus torosus.

- Tyrannosaurs arrived on the scene late in the evolution of dinosaurs. They evolved only during the last 30 million years of the 140-million-year, dinosaur-dominated Mesozoic Era. T. rex was one of the last dinosaurs. Its remains are found close to the Cretaceous-Tertiary Boundary – the timeline some 65 million years ago when dinosaurs disappeared and the Mesozoic ended. Albertosaurus is older than T. rex, living from about 78 to 68 million years ago.
- Fossils of tyrannosaurs are found throughout the northern hemisphere.

Not all dinosaurs lived at the same time. The Mesozoic Era lasted for 150 million years. Allosaurus and Stegosaurus appeared about halfway through (156-145 million years ago).

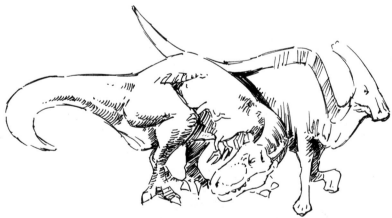

Albertosaurus and its prey, Parasaurolophus, appeared 78 million years ago.

By the time Tyrannosaurus rex and Triceratops arrived on the dinosaur scene 68 million years ago, dinosaur days were numbered.

• Tyrannosaurs were formidable hunters. Like many modern predators, their overlapping vision enabled them to accurately measure distances and to pick out camouflaged or moving prey. Long, complex nasal passages in the fossil skulls with corresponding, well-developed olfactory regions in tyrannosaur brain cases indicate a keen sense of smell. Once they pinpointed potential meals, long, powerful legs enabled them to give chase, possibly reaching speeds of up to 40 kilometres per hour – as fast as a coyote can run. Strong neck muscles and powerful jaws helped these fierce predators drive their knife-like teeth through the flesh and bones of prey. It is estimated that, from the likely size and strength of the neck and jaws muscles, an adult T. rex would have easily been able to rip 100 kilograms of meat off a carcass with one bite – approximately the weight of one large man – and possibly as much as 200 kilograms (two large men). The human weight equivalent would be for the same large man to eat three medium-sized pizzas in one bite.

- Full-grown tyrannosaurs ranged in size from eight to 13 metres in length – about the length of eight adult humans lined up head-to-toe. The largest tyrannosaur was T. rex. An adult albertosaur skeleton is about three metres shorter and more lightly built than an adult T. rex. The specimen found at Dinosaur Provincial Park in 1991 was small even for Albertosaurus.

An adult human would have been a tasty morsel for an adult Tyrannosaurus rex, an adult Albertosaurus or even the juvenile Albertosaurus.

- The first Albertosaurus was found in 1884 by geologist Joseph B. Tyrrell near the present-day Royal Tyrrell Museum of Palaeontology. Tyrrell was looking at coal seams in the Red Deer River badlands for the Geological Survey of Canada when he came face to face with the 70-million-year-old dinosaur skull. Although not an expert on dinosaurs, he realized the skull was important and should be preserved. He and his companions loaded it onto a cart for the slow journey to Fort Calgary. From there, it was shipped to Ottawa.

• Almost from the time Albertosaurus was first described and named, scientists have been assigning it and reassigning it new names. Even now, some scientists contend that the tyrannosaurus of Dinosaur Provincial Park are a separate genus from those found in later sediments, and should be called Gorgosaurus, as had been proposed in 1914.

Parental Care

For many years, scientists based their theories of dinosaur birth and parental care on the behaviour of modern reptiles. Then, in the late 1970s, one of the world's best dinosaur nest sites was found in Montana. The eggs and embryos belong to the hadrosaur called Maiasaura. In the mid-1980s, Canada's first dinosaur egg site was discovered in an area called Devil's Coulee near Warner, Alberta. The site contains the remains of nest sites of Hypacrosaurus, another kind of hadrosaur. Also found was a single nest of the small, predatory dinosaur **Troodon**, identifiable by embryos fossilized within similar eggs found elsewhere.

More recently, in China's Gobi Desert, the skeleton of an **Oviraptor**, a theropod dinosaur long believed to eat dinosaur eggs, was found atop a nest of fossil eggs. Analysis of embryos within the same kind of eggs indicate that they are unhatched Oviraptor eggs. Scientists now believe the dinosaur was protecting her nest when a sandstorm buried her alive.

Newly hatched and young tyrannosaurs may have required care by their parents to survive. Successful stalking and hunting are complex skills and take time to learn. Today, many carnivores tend their young for the first part of their lives, and during that time, the juveniles learn to hunt and fend for themselves.

GEOLOGICAL SURVEY OF CANADA

J.B. Tyrrell came west in the 1880s to survey coal seams in the Drumheller valley for the Geological Survey of Canada. He is the first person on record to find the remains of Albertosaurus.

D.L. SLOAN '95 ©

Oviraptor's reputation as a nest-raiding egg-eater was changed to that of a caring parent when scientists found a specimen atop a nest of Oviraptor eggs in the Gobi desert. The position of the fossil dinosaur suggests it was trying to protect its eggs when a sandstorm overwhelmed it.

Part 2

Life near the Nest

The *Albertosaurus* was one hatchling in a nest of young dinosaurs.

They were always hungry. Every time their mother checked the nest, she and her siblings cried for food. They devoured the meat their mother brought them, picking clean the bones of a three-tonne hadrosaur in days. Scratching with her claws and nipping with her fingernail-sized teeth, the young *Albertosaurus* snatched food from brothers and sisters, eating more than her share – only the strongest and most aggressive ate well.

Life was uncertain for the young dinosaurs during their first weeks. One egg never hatched. The mother accidentally stepped on one youngster with her huge, clawed, three-toed foot. The smallest, weakest youngsters starved because they couldn't compete for food. The surviving siblings crowded the dead dinosaurs out of the nest.

The mother couldn't protect the nest all of the time; she had to hunt to feed them, leaving the babies vulnerable. One was snatched from above, carried off in the jaws of a giant *Quetzalcoatlus.*

At one month old, the young *Albertosaurus* and her siblings were active and curious. They investigated every moving insect, every squawk of a bird from the trees, every part of the clearing that was their home and the bush around it.

They wrestled, rolling and tumbling in the dirt, battling one another for possession of bones and sticks. They stalked, ambushed and chased one another, playing today the skills they would need as adults.

It was play that led the young dinosaurs to their first real battle.

The young *Albertosaurus* and her siblings were chasing each other in an antic race in and out of the trees, the youngsters flowing back and forth and around as the pursued suddenly pivotted as a pack and become pursuers, and those who had been at the rear were swept along in the changeable tide. Toothy jaws wide, the young predators almost barked with excitement.

Suddenly, with the young *Albertosaurus* gaining the lead, they ran right into the midst of a large pack of dromaeosaurs feeding on the remains of a young hadrosaur.

The lead albertosaurs skidded to an abrupt halt and froze, their siblings behind piling up in momentary confusion. For one single, startled moment, the two groups of dinosaurs – one with size and ferociousness on its side, the other with speed, numbers and an arsenal of killing claws – looked at each other, eyes wide in surprise.

Then instinct took over.

The albertosaurs exploded in a raging, roaring assault of teeth and viciousness. The dromaeosaurs launched themselves towards the larger intruders, shrieking in fury, with jaws snapping and claws extended to rip and tear.

A dromaeosaur leapt onto the young *Albertosaurus'* shoulders, and she felt its teeth clamp onto her neck and its deadly claws rake the flesh over her ribs. She twisted her head, grabbed its long, stiff tail in her teeth and tore the animal from her back, whipping it around into a tree. Pain, the stench of blood and the deafening noise enraged her further.

With a vicious shake of her head, the *Albertosaurus* snapped the spine of another dromaeosaur and looked around, intent on finding another. Through the trees, she spotted slender, agile forms matching the smaller predators' shape fleeing. Snarling and roaring, she gave chase, intent on the kill. The dromaeosaurs were too quick – with their head start, they outstripped the larger, taller *Albertosaurus*. The red fog gradually receded from her vision, and, through the trees around her, she noticed siblings who, like her, had pursued the smaller predators.

The young dinosaur returned to the scene of the fight. Crumpled bodies lay upon the ground. She made out the figures of injured brothers and sisters.

Walking over to a hurt sibling, she bent and sniffed at the wounds. Gently, the young *Albertosaurus* nudged her sister's shoulder with her snout. There was no response.

Four albertosaurs were on the ground, two with deep gashes in their abdomens. Almost three times that many dromaeosaurs were strewn about. Turning, the young *Albertosaurus* bent to examine one of the bodies. The dromaeosaur was panting and trembling in pain, and able only to twitch its limbs. Unconcerned, the larger dinosaur dragged at it with her foot, and turning it over, bit into the exposed belly and fed.

Philip Currie measures exposed bones while a technician records data. The information will be used to determine the approximate age of the dinosaur when it died.

FROM FIELD TO MUSEUM

ONCE THE EXTENT AND POSITION OF THE SKELETON had been determined, crews started **trenching** around the specimen. Because the *Albertosaurus* skeleton was too large to be removed in a single block, the crew separated it into five sections. These were then covered with paper and jacketed in layers of burlap soaked in plaster. In the larger blocks, wooden splints were set into the jackets to keep them from sagging

After determining its position in the ground, field crews dig trenches around the specimen (above). Layers of burlap and plaster protect the fossil block. Crews gradually undercut the fossils, plastering as they go, until the specimen is a giant plaster and rock mushroom that can be flipped over (left). The exposed side is then jacketed.

and breaking apart during the trip to the Royal Tyrrell Museum.

By mid-August, the dinosaur was ready to be moved from where it had rested for 75 million years.

However, there was a small, 800-kilogram problem. The largest fossil block, containing the skull and torso, was so big only a bulldozer could move it. Earth-mover companies across southern Alberta were contacted. One bid was so low, the collecting crew had doubts that the contractor had a machine large enough and powerful enough to move the block. When the contractor showed up, he was driving a huge tractor, complete with a 60,000-kilogram winch with enough power to move 50 fossil blocks at once.

The block was loaded into a dumpster, a container large enough and sturdy enough to contain

While crews were able to carry the smaller specimen blocks out of Little Sandhill Coulee, it took a bulldozer to move the block that contained the dinosaur's trunk and head.

and support the specimen during its journey out of Little Sandhill Coulee. The contractor hitched the dumpster to his winch, and began the slow trek over the badlands, dragging the Museum's rock-, fossil- and-plaster prize.

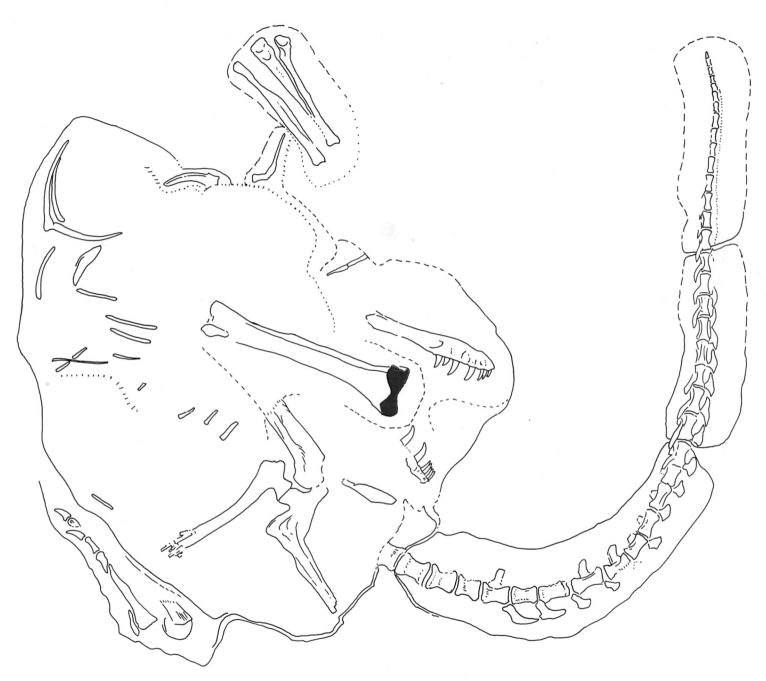

When a specimen is excavated, its position in the ground is mapped. Because the skeleton was so large, technicians separated it into five blocks to protect it and facilitate its removal from the quarry. The quarry map shows the Albertosaurus' tail alone consisted of three of those blocks. The bone that is highlighted is the ankle bone that first caught Philip Currie's attention.

Seventy-five million years after they were buried, a technician slowly removes rock from the young dinosaur's bones.

FRAGILE BONES

ONCE THE YOUNG DINOSAUR ARRIVED AT THE Museum, the painstaking task of removing everything but bones began. The amount of information obtained from a fossil depends largely on how carefully it is prepared.

When working with fossilized bones – especially theropod bones, which are hollow like bird bones – extreme caution is required. Breaks and fractures can happen with just tiny amounts of

By examining a dinosaur's complete skull, palaeontologists can determine the animal's species, diet and relative intelligence compared to other dinosaurs.

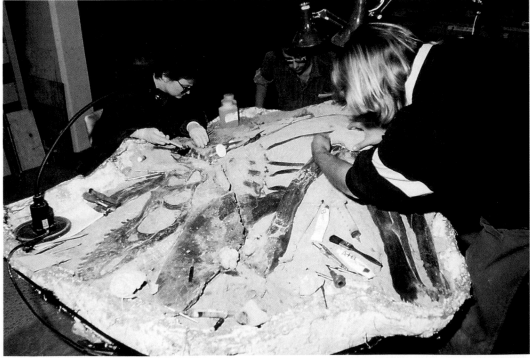

It took technicians more than five years to prepare the specimen. Because of the importance of so many features of the skeleton, many of the bones had to be removed from the matrix and prepared completely for research and illustration.

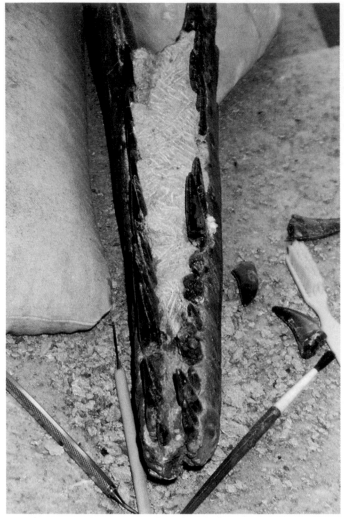

Albertosaurus' lower jaw is normally long and very narrow. Measuring only four centimetres at the front, the lower jaw of the young dinosaur was compressed slightly during fossilization.

Debate about how to best preserve and display the exceptional skeleton of the juvenile Albertosaurus went on for months. Museum Director Bruce Naylor settled the question – the bones were too fragile and the specimen too valuable to risk damage in a three-dimensional display.

pressure. The young *Albertosaurus'* bones were extremely fragile. Although they were well fossilized, the brittle exteriors hid insides that were chalky and crumbly.

Technicians planned on removing all the bones from the rock to produce a three-dimensional exhibit. However, after months of preparation, it was found that the bones were too fragile for this kind of display. It was decided that the specimen would be set into a supporting backdrop and displayed as a panel.

Fossil Formation

Palaeontology is the study of fossils – the remains and traces of ancient life.

Specific conditions must be present at the time of death for an animal or a plant to be fossilized. Many dinosaur fossils in Alberta are found buried in the hardened sands of ancient rivers. In order for a skeleton to remain intact during fossilization, high rates of sediment accumulation in rivers and streams must quickly cover carcasses and protect them from currents, scavengers and other things that scatter and deteriorate bones. If burial is quick and complete, impressions of the animal's skin may be preserved.

Replacement, a fossilization process that must occur for bones to be preserved, happens when the organic minerals that make up bone are replaced with non-organic compounds.

Another process, called permineralization, occurs when porous spaces in an animal's bones fill with minerals from groundwater.

Three Steps to Fossilization

(1) After an animal dies, its carcass is quickly buried by sediments. Prior to burial, the bones may be displaced or disarticulated by scavengers or flowing water.

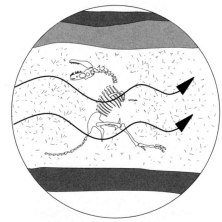

(2) As time passes, organic compounds in the bones are replaced by inorganic minerals. Minerals in groundwater flowing through the sediments may fill the porous spaces within the bones.

(3) Erosion exposes part of the skeleton. Almost all specimens collected are found because of exposed fossils.

Piecing Together Clues: Albertosaurus' World

"You are a detective investigating a murder. The evidence is 75 million years old, some of it has been tampered with, some of it has been lost... and there are no witnesses." This is how palaeontologist Philip Currie describes his job of making sense of a world long past. "Using the clues we find, we try to understand what happened, how it happened and why."

Fortunately, Dinosaur Provincial Park's fossil record has been the focus of research for years. Based on evidence gleaned from the rocks there, we know the young Albertosaurus lived on a wide, flat coastal plain between an inland sea to the east and highlands to the west. The land was swampy, dotted with stands of forest on higher ground and crossed by many streams and rivers.

Family groups of duckbilled Corythosaurus, Lambeosaurus and Parasaurolophus would have browsed on the tough greenery of ferns, leafy trees and flowering plants growing on the plain.

Palaeontologist Philip Currie studies more than the bones of ancient animals – he and the scientists he works with examine sediments, microfossils and all other associated materials found at a quarry to better understand the world in which the animal lived.

Fossil remains indicate that solitary anklyosaurs kept to higher ground and browsed on soft, low-growing horsetails, ferns and bushes. The bony plates that covered the backs and heads of these low-slung, armoured dinosaurs kept them safe from predators. Some species had bony clubs at the end of their tails to further discourage hungry hunters.

Ceratopsian dinosaurs Centrosaurus, Styracosaurus and Chasmosaurus appear to have lived in wetland areas where they could feed on rushes, water lilies and other low-growing plants in marshes and swamps. A five-year survey of horned-dinosaur bonebeds in southern Alberta by Royal Tyrrell Museum of Palaeontology scientists Dave Eberth and Don Brinkman suggests some ceratopsian species migrated seasonally from the coastal plain to avoid the winter storms that flooded wetlands. Every so often, an especially bad storm developed while the herds travelled. Rivers overflowed and spread across the land, trapping animals on the plain. The huge bonebeds found scattered across southern Alberta are the jumbled remains of thousands of horned dinosaurs.

Albertosaurus shared the position of top carnivore in the Dinosaur Provincial Park area with fellow-tyrannosaur Daspletosaurus. The young albertosaur would have helped cull the populations of herbivorous dinosaurs – chasing down hadrosaurs and young or weak horned dinosaurs for food. She probably would have also scavenged dead animals for food whenever she found them.

Smaller dinosaurs shared the lowland habitat with the young Albertosaurus. The toothless bird-mimic dinosaurs, ornithomimids, probably fed on insects, eggs, fruits, seeds and small animals. Troodon may have been the Cretaceous equivalent of today's coyote. Its relatively large brain, enormous eyes with stereoscopic vision, hands with opposable digits and body built for speed and agility would have helped it hunt small animals for food. Troodon probably ate whatever it could catch or find. **Dromaeosaurs**, bigger-clawed and shorter-legged than **troodontids**, were also present in Dinosaur Provincial Park.

Other animals of Late Cretaceous Alberta included birds, pterosaurs and crocodiles. Narrow-jawed champsosaurs lived on river and stream banks, fishing for frogs, turtles and fish in the water, and ancestors of today's Komodo dragon – the monitor lizards – scavenged and hunted on land. Mammals were small, nocturnal, shrew-like creatures that fed on fruit, seeds and insects.

Evidence of our ancient world is often poorly preserved. Scientists can never be certain how much information they'll obtain from a fossil and its quarry. Each fossil found adds to scientists' knowledge of prehistoric animals, environments and climates.

Part 3

The Hunt

By the time they were two months old, the *Albertosaurus* and her siblings followed their mother everywhere. Although they had grown quickly, next to their mother they were small and wiry. Like all juvenile tyrannosaurs, their legs were long compared to their bodies, allowing them to keep up with her as she searched for prey. The young dinosaurs helped their mother find, stalk and chase their meals, learning by watching her how to judge which prey were worth the effort of bringing them down, and how best to exploit the surrounding environment.

One day, the young *Albertosaurus* and a group of siblings heard intriguing noises from the forest. Drawing closer, they found a squat, armoured dinosaur lumbering through the bush.

Sensing something, the strange dinosaur stopped and lifted its head to sniff the air, marking the presence of the young predators. Wary, but not worried, the animal started grazing on the ferns and club mosses around it, ponderously tearing at the foliage. The young albertosaurs eyed the armoured plates on its back and shoulders, calculating how to make this herbivore their meal.

Quickly, they fanned out, surrounding the small clearing. The ankylosaur tracked their movements with its small eyes. Snorting, it shifted its feet and lifted the large club on the end of its long, stiff tail.

The *Albertosaurus'* younger brother lunged toward the dinosaur, opening his jaws to sever the backbone. The young *Albertosaurus* quickly followed, just as the ankylosaur pivoted and swung its tail. The club hit the brother on the chest, crushing ribs with a crunch. He shrieked and tumbled to the side of the clearing, collapsing in a choking pile as blood poured from his nose.

Desperately, the young *Albertosaurus* leapt to avoid the swinging tail, but it clipped her shin and sent her flying. Her remaining siblings scrambled out of the way and disappeared into the bush. The young *Albertosaurus* staggered to her feet, and, keeping a wary eye on the snorting, enraged ankylosaur, limped after them.

Her brother was dead. She was injured. Hampered by the pain in her leg, she fought to keep up with her family.

A joint injury in the foot may have affected the dinosaur's ability to move around.

Damage to a Dinosaur

Study of the juvenile Albertosaurus' bones during preparation revealed two unusual growths on the right side of the body.

One is a growth on one of the toe bones, which may have affected ligaments in the foot. The second resulted from a broken fibula, the smaller of the two shin bones. This injury occurred while the dinosaur was still alive, because the fracture had partly healed. A bone spur developed at the break, and grew until it rubbed the other shin bone. It probably caused the young animal a great deal of pain.

Both injuries are on the same side of the body, which has led to speculation that both injuries occurred during one incident. Perhaps the young animal had an encounter with a larger predator. Perhaps it was stepped on when it was very young. Perhaps it was hit by an ankylosaur tail club. We will never know for sure how the dinosaur was hurt, or if the injuries were a factor in the animal's early death.

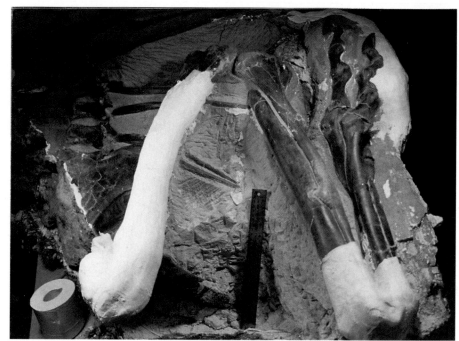

The deforming bone growth on the leg of the juvenile Albertosaurus (see above) may – or may not – have led to the animal's early death. The illustration (below) provides greater detail of the bone spur.

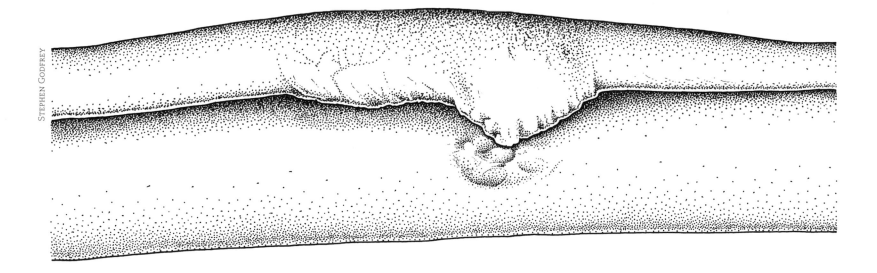

STEPHEN GODFREY

Part 4

Life in the Pack

The young dinosaur's family joined another *Albertosaurus* family. Hunting in a pack meant sharing the meat from each kill among more mouths, but more hunters meant more kills. Almost daily, they brought down an old, a young or an injured plant eater. This eased the pressure on the young *Albertosaurus,* whose leg continued to slow her down.

One evening, as they travelled across their territory, the pack leader suddenly stopped and sniffed the breeze. With the pack, she tracked the scent of long-crested hadrosaurs to a clump of trees upwind. Picking off these herbivores was easier than hunting horned dinosaurs whose long, deadly horns could puncture and pierce a predator's body.

The pack silently approached, watching for weakness, assessing approaches and cutting off escape routes. The adults moved into ambush position on the downwind side of the thicket, while the youngsters stealthily circled around, careful to keep their scent from warning the prey. Slowly, the young predators closed the loop; creeping closer and closer to the unsuspecting herbivores.

A branch snapped. A hadrosaur threw its head up, suddenly alert, moving uneasily. Unable to contain her excitement, the young *Albertosaurus* attacked – roaring, she sprang forward through the trees, followed by the other pack members.

Her biting jaws drew first blood; the small hadrosaur ran, trumpetting in panic, into the jaws of the pack leader. Another albertosaur took down a female, an infant wailing in alarm next to her. The young *Albertosaurus* grabbed it in her teeth and shook it violently. The pack chased the other herbivores as they stampeded blindly away, bringing down another within a few hundred metres. Three herbivores escaped through the forest.

The pack fed well that evening, and settled down to spend the night near the remains of the dead hadrosaurs. Two troodons approached stealthily, eyeing the carcasses, but were warned off by low, rumbling growls. As the sun rose, a single daspletosaur was attracted by the smell of blood. The albertosaur pack sprang up, roaring and posturing, and intimidated the rival.

The season swept on. In the following weeks, the weather cooled and became unpredictable. Brief, torrential rains that had freshened the afternoons became storms that lasted for days. As the days grew shorter, hadrosaur families scattered and horned dinosaurs began the long treks to their wintering grounds in their seasonal herds. With the dispersal of prey, there was little advantage for the large predators to live and hunt in packs; the albertosaur families separated and went their own ways.

Not long after, the young albertosaurs' mother turned against her children as well. Growling and baring her teeth, she chased the young dinosaurs away. It was time for them to find their own hunting territories.

Tyrannosaur Tea Party: How Scientists Think Large Theropods Behaved

Nobody knows exactly how dinosaurs behaved. No palaeontologist can state definitively what they ate, how they cared for their young, how they interacted with others of their species, or how any other dinosaur behaviour took place.

Behaviours do not fossilize, but occasionally evidence of behaviour is preserved. Fossils such as trackways, dung and bite-marked bone are shadows of dinosaur activity preserved in rock, and provide clues to how dinosaurs lived. Scientists supplement these clues in the fossil record with knowledge about how animals behave today. Even then, nothing is certain.

Palaeontologists have long debated what tyrannosaurs ate. Some scientists think they were scavengers – that, like hyenas today, they ate dead animals whose rotting smell would attract them across great distances. The name of Albertosaurus sarcophagus, a close relative to the young dinosaur, reflects this view – the Latin "sarcophagus" translates as "flesh eater." Other scientists believe tyrannosaurs had too many body features typical of active, aggressive hunters to live on only carrion, and question whether the huge meat eaters could have found enough carcasses to keep them fed. Another group of scientists believes tyrannosaurs were opportunists, and ate any meal they could get, fresh or not. Research shows that even hyenas hunt living prey about 30 per cent of the time, and that lions and cougars, which of all modern animals most prefer fresh meat, will eat carrion if they are hungry enough.

Bonebeds also can provide glimpses into dinosaur behaviour. Tyrannosaurs have long been believed by scientists to be loners, only occasionally and briefly coming together in small groups for mating or territorial disputes. However, new data from a bonebed located 60 kilometres from the Royal Tyrrell Museum of Palaeontology are changing these

Part 6

Old Man River

The young *Albertosaurus* was weak. It was weeks since she had eaten enough to feel full and satisfied.

One muggy morning, she drank her fill from a slow, meandering river, then settled herself nearby to rest.

The sun beat down. She drowsed in the heat, and fell asleep.

She never awakened. Her starving body had had enough. By the time the afternoon rains started, she was dead.

She lay there for days, the smell of her body attracting insects and small animals to feed. She gave rise to several generations of blowflies. She fed small lizards and the shrew-like mammals that scurried about at night. Oddly enough, no large scavengers found her carcass, and her skeleton remained intact, slowly being pulled back in an arch by the powerful tendons along the spine.

views. There are about 150 dinosaur bonebeds in Alberta – all but this one are dominated by the remains of herbivorous dinosaurs. This one exception contains the remains of at least 10 albertosaurs that died together 70 million years ago.

Philip Currie, the palaeontologist excavating the site, thinks this may be evidence that these large carnivores spent part of their lives living in groups – perhaps to more effectively hunt the horned dinosaurs that gathered seasonally in huge herds to migrate across Alberta.

Anatomy of a Predator

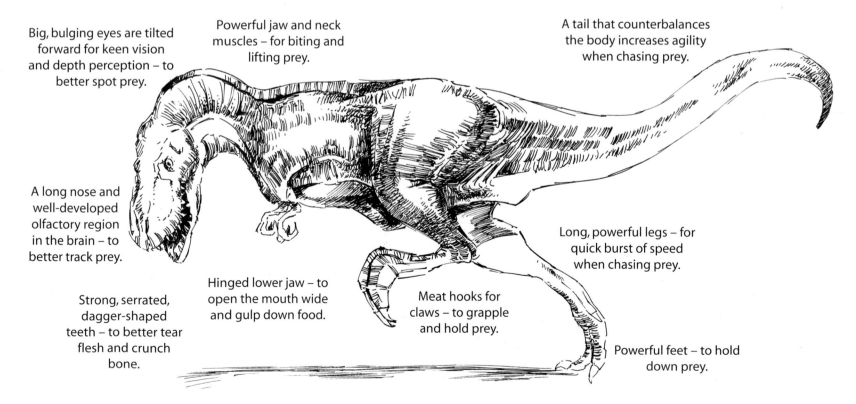

Large brain (compared to other animals of the same period) – to better outsmart prey.

Big, bulging eyes are tilted forward for keen vision and depth perception – to better spot prey.

Powerful jaw and neck muscles – for biting and lifting prey.

A tail that counterbalances the body increases agility when chasing prey.

A long nose and well-developed olfactory region in the brain – to better track prey.

Long, powerful legs – for quick burst of speed when chasing prey.

Strong, serrated, dagger-shaped teeth – to better tear flesh and crunch bone.

Hinged lower jaw – to open the mouth wide and gulp down food.

Meat hooks for claws – to grapple and hold prey.

Powerful feet – to hold down prey.

Part 5

Life Alone

In her search for territory, the lone *Albertosaurus* fought many competitors, and lost to them all. She was chased away from the best hunting grounds by bigger, more aggressive albertosaurs. She was forced to retreat from the territories of daspletosaurs. She even had to give up meals when confronted by large packs of dromaeosaurs. She sneaked and skulked and retreated, too small and too inexperienced to compete.

The pain in her leg continued. Although she could walk and run, the injury slowed her down, and caused her further disadvantage in both battles to establish turf and the hunt. She caught little live prey; her diet consisted mostly of carrion – dead animals whose smell attracted her, and many other carnivores, across great distances.

She found the stinking carcass of a *Chasmosaurus* in a field one day. The five troodons feeding on it reluctantly moved away as she roared and advanced on them, but did not go far. They knew the young scavenger, with her large jaw and uneven bite, could not eat every scrap of meat, and there would be leftovers.

The body was putrid and crawling with maggots, but the *Albertosaurus* did not hesitate. She wolfed down the best meal she had had in many weeks. She stuck her head into the great body cavity and gulped down the guts; she tore mouthfuls of meat from the muscular haunches, swallowing them whole. As she stripped long muscles off the legs, an enormous roar echoed behind her. Startled, she swung around, baring her teeth, and snarled back. Striding towards her was a large, heavy-set, adult albertosaur, drawn to the clearing, as she had been, by the sweet smell of rotting flesh. The young *Albertosaurus* roared, shaking her head, at the rival for her dinner. In her peripheral vision, she noticed the quiet retreat of the troodons. Determined to win this fight, the *Albertosaurus* stood in front of the carcass, pulling herself up to her greatest height. Even then, she was only two-thirds the size of the adult.

The older animal charged, mouth open to bite, and the young dinosaur leaped aside and turned to confront her rival again. The adult swung its head, trying again to bite the younger scavenger, but the young dinosaur, though smaller, again jumped out of the way. The third attack by the larger dinosaur caught the *Albertosaurus* in the side, momentarily knocking the wind out of her before instinct took over and she turned and ran. The older animal chased her briefly before turning back to feed on the *Chasmosaurus*.

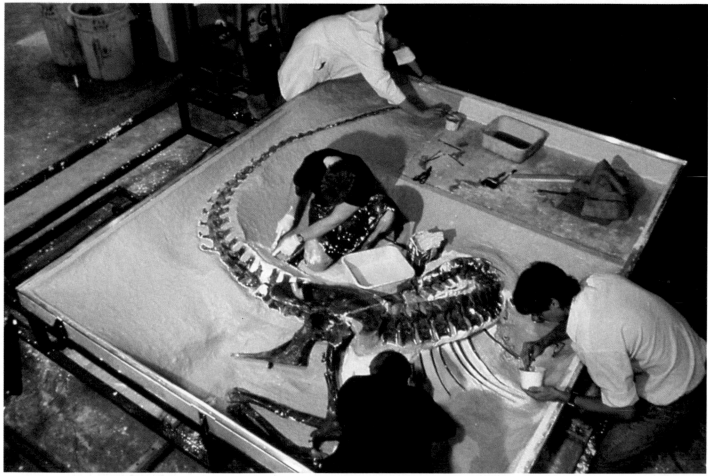

Museum technicians worked through the night to finish the specimen for display.

DISPLAY

THE FIELD CREW HAD DISCOVERED THE JUVENILE *Albertosaurus* skeleton left side up. However, the right side of the body is displayed because that side is in better condition. Some bones – the right ribs, right arm and leg – stand free of the rock, each supported only by thin metal brackets. The fractured right fibula was returned to its natural position; if you look closely at the mount, you can see the bone spur and the hole in the tibia.

Each of the bones that stands free of the panel is supported by a thin, steel bracket, cut and welded to fit the bones exactly.

To create a backdrop that complements the dark, glossy bones, technicians brought sandstone from the original quarry, ground it up and glued the sand on the background of the fibreglass and plaster panel.

In the final push to finish the display before the glaziers sealed the specimen into its case, technicians worked through the night, touching up the backdrop and making sure the fragile bones were secure. At about 3:00 A.M., one technician inadvertently brushed his hand against the dinosaur's ribs. There was a loud "crack!" Everyone froze. Then Darren Tanke looked up and calmly said, "That didn't sound good."

Even with the steel brackets supporting them, the thin bones of the ribcage were so brittle the slightest pressure caused them to break.

In minutes, the damage was repaired, leaving no evidence.

But when the glaziers arrived to cover the display, Tanke had to leave the room. "I couldn't watch," he says. "One slip and that 200-kilogram sheet of glass would have smashed everything."

The workers lowered the two-centimetre-thick glass panel onto the display without incident, and the skeleton was sealed into its case, protected from dust and the damaging effects of changing humidity in the gallery.

The Death Pose

No one knows what led to the early death of the young dinosaur, but scientists can piece together what happened soon after it died. With no resistance by muscles or gravity, the strong ropes of tendons lining the backbone pulled the young dinosaur's head and tail back into a tight arch. As the body dried, the tendons lost elasticity and locked the Albertosaurus' skeleton in position.

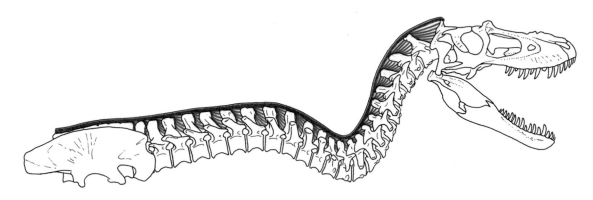

The tendons lining the spine are thick, elastic ropes holding the vertebrae in place. When an animal dies, these tissues contract and pull the body into a backward arch. As muscles and ligaments deteriorate, resistance lessens; the arch tightens.

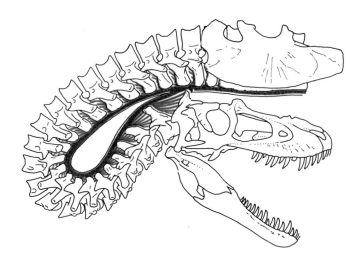

Part 6

Old Man River

The young *Albertosaurus* was weak. It was weeks since she had eaten enough to feel full and satisfied.

One muggy morning, she drank her fill from a slow, meandering river, then settled herself nearby to rest.

The sun beat down. She drowsed in the heat, and fell asleep.

She never awakened. Her starving body had had enough. By the time the afternoon rains started, she was dead.

She lay there for days, the smell of her body attracting insects and small animals to feed. She gave rise to several generations of blowflies. She fed small lizards and the shrew-like mammals that scurried about at night. Oddly enough, no large scavengers found her carcass, and her skeleton remained intact, slowly being pulled back in an arch by the powerful tendons along the spine.

One day, the afternoon rains did not stop. The wind picked up, flattened the horsetails and ferns along the bank and howled through the trees, pulling off branches and blowing rain sideways. Water poured from the sky.

The level of water in the riverbed rose. It flowed past the dinosaur, and still it rose.

When the bank overflowed, the young *Albertosaurus'* body lifted and floated down river. Her left arm remained embedded in the root-bound sand where she had died. The current tugged the carcass along until it filled with water. As she sank, the flow turned her body over so it came to rest on its right side. The current pulled the left leg up and over the back. As the sand-laden water swirled around the dinosaur, the contorted body slowed the current, allowing sand and silt to cover the body. All was buried except the left foot.

The storm ended and the water level began to drop. As the foot swayed in the sinking current, first the toes, then the long bones of the sole, dropped off and were carried a short distance from the carcass. Then they, too, were covered with sand.

Part 7

Second Life

Seventy-six million years later, erosion of the sandstone that entombed the young dinosaur exposed the boot-like end of her pubic bone. Rain, freezing water, changes in temperature and humidity during the following seasons worked at the exposed bone, fracturing and reducing it to fragments.

Some years later, rain from a brief summer storm poured down the shallow slope, washing away the last gritty, soft layer of sandstone that covered the dinosaur's left ankle bone.

The astragalus was exposed, and the young *Albertosaurus* was about to embark on the next stage of her journey through time….

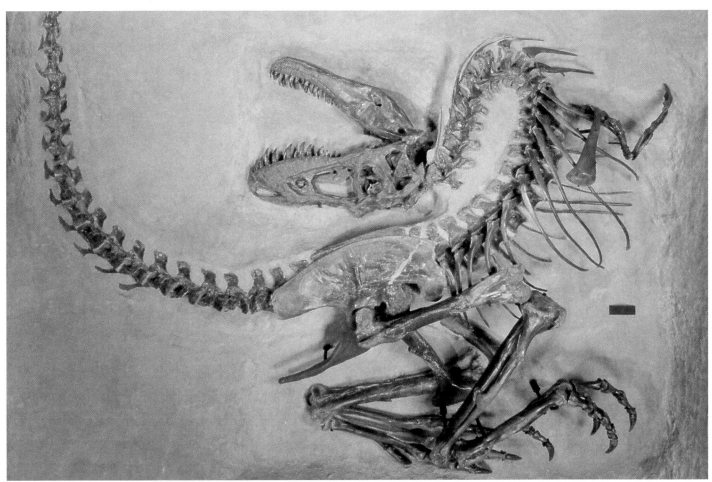

Sealed behind glass, the juvenile Albertosaurus is a striking display of an original fossil.

IN THE GALLERY

EARLY IN 1997, THE JUVENILE ALBERTOSAURUS made its debut in the Royal Tyrrell Museum of Palaeontology's Gallery. The result of five years of preparation work is a beautiful panel presenting the young dinosaur in the position in which it was found in 1991.

Glossary

ARTICULATED: United by means of a joint. An articulated skeleton is one in which the bones are in place in relation to one another.

ASTRAGALUS: One of the ankle bones.

BADLANDS: Terrain distinguished by hoodoos, sinkholes and features of rapid erosion.

BONEBED: The jumbled remains of many animals.

CARRION: Dead flesh.

CERATOPSIAN: An herbivorous dinosaur characterized by horns on its face.

CHAMPSOSAUR: A crocodile-like reptile that existed until 50 million years ago.

DROMAEOSAUR: A small, meat-eating dinosaur characterized by a sickle-shaped claw on the second toe of each hind foot.

FOSSIL: Remains and traces of ancient life. To be classified as a fossil, a specimen must be at least 10,000 years old.

GENUS: A grouping of related species.

HADROSAUR: An herbivorous dinosaur characterized by a duck-like bill and numerous grinding teeth.

MESOZOIC ERA: Period of time from 205 million to 65 million years ago, during which dinosaurs evolved and became dominant terrestrial animals.

MONITOR LIZARD: A carnivorous lizard up to three metres in length. Modern monitors include Indonesia's Komodo dragon.

MONSOON: The season of heavy winter rains.

OLFACTORY: Pertaining to the sense of smell.

OPPORTUNISTIC: Taking advantage of circumstances as they present themselves.

ORNITHOMIMID: A theropod dinosaur with long legs and a long neck. It had no teeth and is believed to have eaten insects, eggs and small animals.

OVERBURDEN: The rock above a specimen that must be removed in order to expose and collect the specimen.

PALAEONTOLOGY: The study of ancient life through fossils.

PERMINERALIZATION: A fossilization process by which ground water minerals fill porous spaces within bone and wood.

PTEROSAURS: Flying reptiles of the Mesozoic Era.

REPLACEMENT: A fossilization process by which organic minerals within bone are replaced by inorganic compounds.

SCAVENGER: An animal that eats animals that are already dead.

THEROPODS: Meat-eating dinosaurs.

TRENCHING: Digging a ditch.

TROODONTID: A member of the troodontae family of dinosaurs – small theropods who are believed to have been among the smartest of the dinosaurs.

TYRANNOSAUR: A large meat-eating dinosaur, characterized by two fingers on its short front limbs.

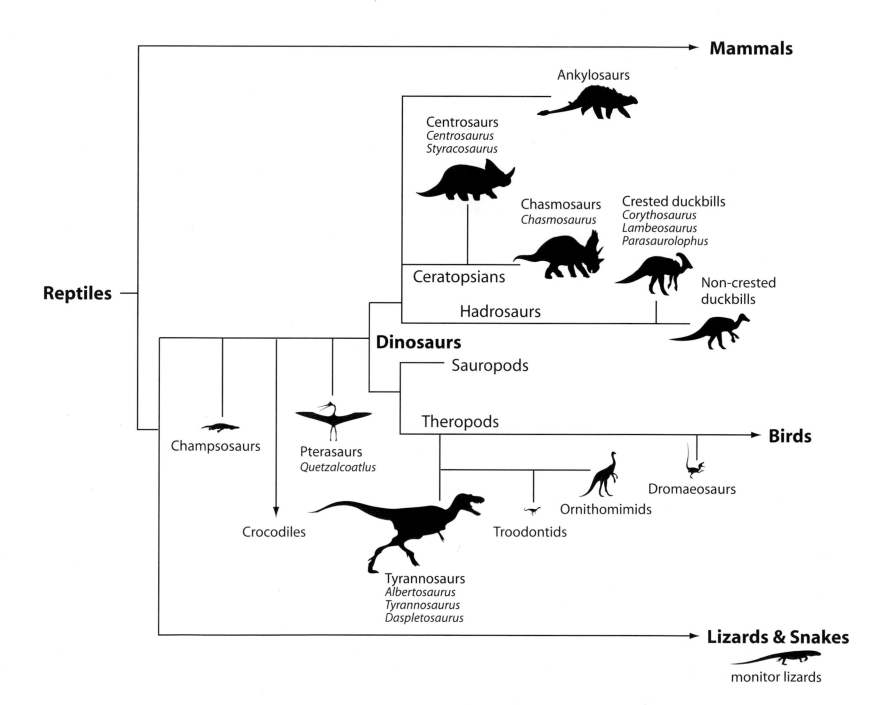

Mammals

Ankylosaurs

Centrosaurs
Centrosaurus
Styracosaurus

Chasmosaurs
Chasmosaurus

Crested duckbills
Corythosaurus
Lambeosaurus
Parasaurolophus

Ceratopsians

Non-crested
duckbills

Hadrosaurs

Reptiles

Dinosaurs

Sauropods

Theropods

Birds

Champsosaurs

Pterasaurs
Quetzalcoatlus

Dromaeosaurs

Ornithomimids

Crocodiles

Troodontids

Tyrannosaurs
Albertosaurus
Tyrannosaurus
Daspletosaurus

Lizards & Snakes

monitor lizards

LINDA MOORE

PHILIP CURRIE first decided to become a palaeontologist when he found a plastic dinosaur in a cereal box when he was 6 years old. He collected all of the dinosaurs that the cereal company was giving out, with the exception of the Tyrannosaurus rex model – which, he says, may be why, more than 40 years later, he is still looking for tyrannosaurs. Recently, he has been studying feathered-dinosaur specimens from China, and excavating an historic Albertosaurus bonebed on the Red Deer River.

DAVE EBERTH is sedimentary geologist at the Royal Tyrrell Museum. Projects include dating the sediments of Dinosaur Provincial Park to 76.5 million to 74.5 million years ago by measuring radiometric isotopes, initiating the Museum's Field Experience program in which members of the public dig up fossils alongside Museum scientists, and conducting the survey of horned-dinosaur bonebeds in southern Alberta that shed light on Alberta's Late Cretaceous climate and on ceratopsian herding and migration patterns.

KATHY SIMPKINS

Vertebrate palaeontologist DON BRINKMAN is the Royal Tyrrell Museum's curator of terrestrial non-dinosaurian vertebrates. He studies crocodiles, champsosaurs and other forms of ancient life that lived on land during the time of the dinosaurs, and frequently reminds staff at the Museum that more than dinosaurs lived during the Cretaceous Period. However, his true professional love is turtles. Brinkman likes to cite how, in 1998, the Chicago Museum of Natural History paid US$8.3 Million for a turtle fossil that happened to have the T. rex named Sue mixed up in the same matrix.

DARREN TANKE started in palaeontology as a field volunteer with the Provincial Museum of Alberta's Dinosaur Program, working with Philip Currie on excavations in Dinosaur Provincial Park in 1979. His volunteer work and passion for dinosaurs led to a full-time position as palaeontology technician with the Royal Tyrrell Museum in 1987. In addition to being one of the people who discovered the juvenile *Albertosaurus* in 1991, Tanke was its chief preparator.

The Royal Tyrrell Museum houses more than 100,000 fossils in its collection. About 800 specimens and more than 40 complete dinosaur skeletons are displayed.

THE JUVENILE ALBERTOSAURUS AT HOME

VISIT THE ROYAL TYRRELL MUSEUM OF Palaeontology, and see the juvenile *Albertosaurus* for yourself.

Located in the middle of the Red Deer River badlands where so many dinosaur bones and other fossils have come to light during the last century, the Royal Tyrrell Museum is well situated to showcase spectacular fossils such as this. More than 40 complete dinosaur skeletons are displayed – one of the largest collections under one roof anywhere. Some were collected from the hills outside the Museum; many others come from Dinosaur Provincial Park, further down the Red Deer River.

Other familiar creatures awaiting you at the Museum are giant flying reptile *Quetzalcoatlus* soaring above the jumbled remains of hundreds of horned dinosaurs; long-crested *Parasaurolophus* emerging from the rock; and horned

A toothy Albertosaurus, *created by sculptor Brian Cooley, greets visitors to the Royal Tyrrell Museum. Sculptures of dinosaurs complement the museum's exhibits of dinosaur skeletons such as Triceratops (lower right) and Albertosaurus (upper right).*

Every year, hundreds of thousands of visitors from around the world come to the Royal Tyrrell Museum to see its exhibits and learn about the mysterious creatures that once inhabited our planet.

dinosaur *Centrosaurus*, whose carcass feeds *Albertosaurus* and *Dromaeosaurus* alike.

As a world-class exhibition and research centre, the Museum does more than showcase dinosaurs. It exhibits the history of life in all its forms, from the beginning of multicellular life 3.5 billion years ago to the arrival of humans in North America 15,000 years ago. Its curators study invertebrates, plants, fish, marine reptiles, lizards, turtles, mammals and many other creatures, as well as the environments in which they once lived and are found today. They are supported by a team of technicians, illustrators, collections managers and, during the summer field season, by volunteers who come from around the world to help them prospect and excavate specimens throughout southern Alberta.

More than 350,000 visitors come to the Museum each year. They explore the displays, take part in dynamic interpretive programs and catch tantalizing glimpses into current palaeontologist research.